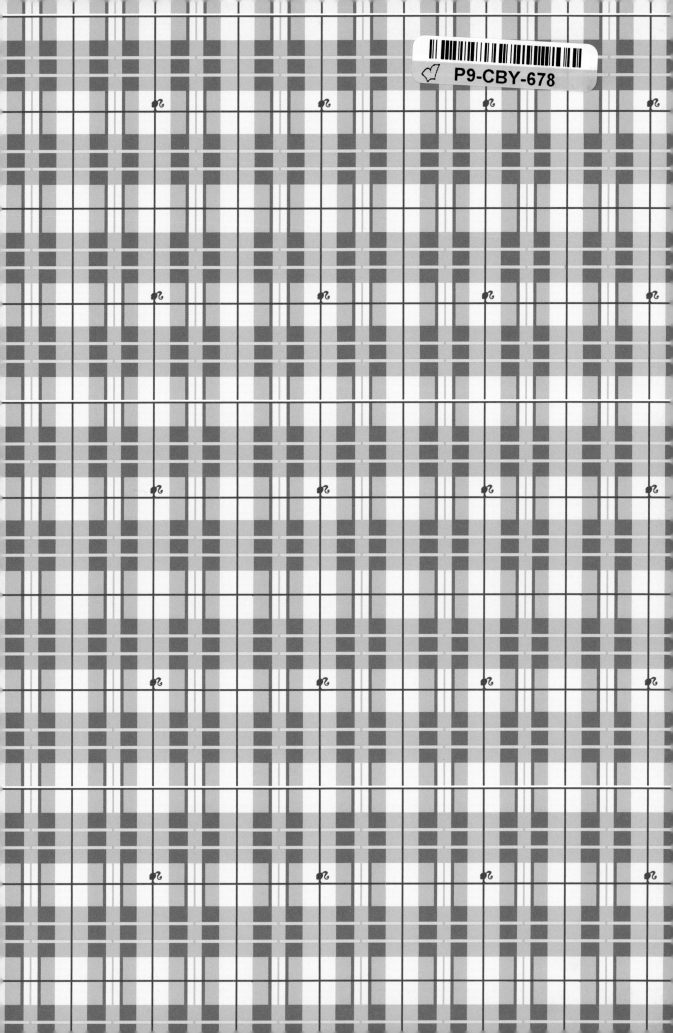

Bath • New York • Singapore • Hong Kong • Cologne • Delhi
Melbourne • Amsterdam • Johannesburg • Auckland • Shenzhen

The super-glam Princess Charm School parade starts on TV as Blair Willows gets home from work. Her little sister, Emily, has made paper tiaras to watch the show! Blair thinks it's sweet that Emily loves princesses, but she knows it's a dream world away from their small apartment in Gardania and her daily work in the café.

It's time for the Princess Charm School lottery! Although the school is for royal girls, every year an ordinary girl wins the chance to become a Lady Royal. Blair is the winner – Emily entered her in the draw! Blair can't believe it, but wants to help her mother and her little sister so agrees to go. A second later, a fabulous carriage arrives to take Blair to Princess Charm School.

Blair Willows wins!

Princess Charm School is wonderfully grand and sparkles brightly in the sun. Glittery sprites fly by and students hurry to class. Blair feels a bit nervous and is not sure where to go.

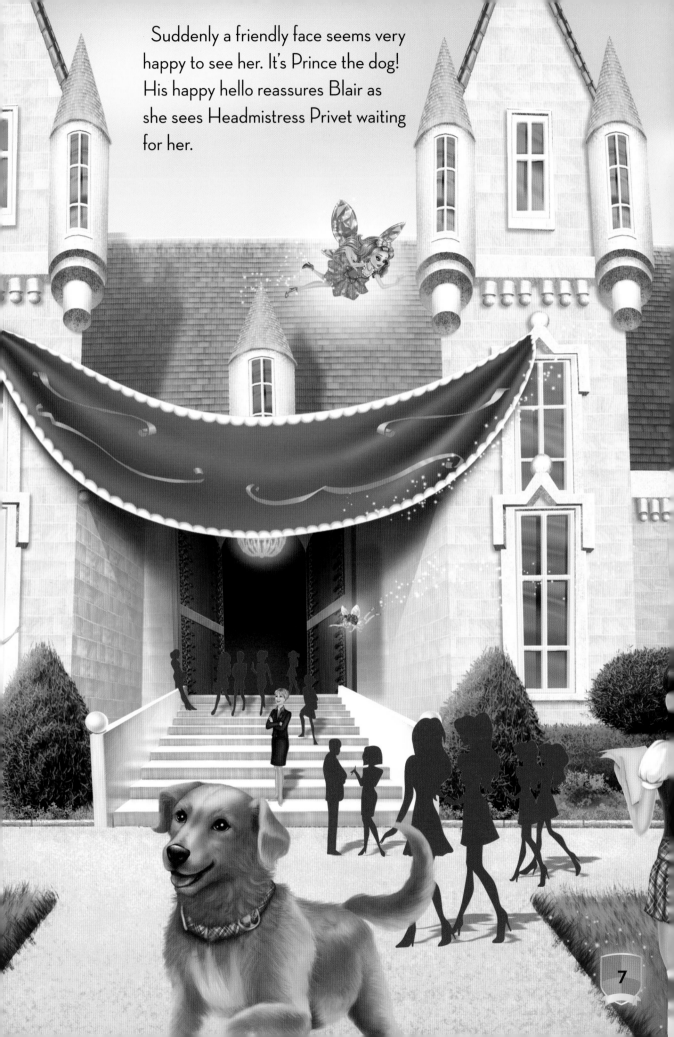

Suddenly a friendly face seems very happy to see her. It's Prince the dog! His happy hello reassures Blair as she sees Headmistress Privet waiting for her.

Headmistress Privet welcomes Blair to Princess Charm School and takes her to a locker in the glitzy modern wing of the school. She tells Blair that only a few lottery girls make it to graduation and asks if she is up to the task. Blair replies that she'll do her best because she wants to make life better for her little sister and her mother.

They take a tour of the school and Blair is caught up in the beauty and excitement of everything around her.

Blair's personal Princess Assistant, Piper the sprite, helps Blair go through her locker, which is filled with dazzling princess accessories. Blair meets her new roommates, Isla and Hadley, two potential princesses. They are really friendly and invite Blair to hang out. A girl called Delancy and some of the other royal girls are not so nice, but Blair doesn't mind because Isla and Hadley are so lovely.

The three new friends sit together for their first class. Dame Devin, their teacher, reminds everyone that she is the sister-in-law of Queen Isabella who sadly died with her family in an accident. Dame Devin's daughter, Delancy, will be the new ruler of Gardania after she graduates. Isla and Hadley whisper to Blair about a legendary magical crown. They think there's something mysterious about the accident...

Dame Devin teaches the class about poise and dance. The girls practise gliding gracefully around the room. Blair finds it difficult at first, but tries hard and realizes she can do it! Delancy is jealous of her success and sneakily trips Blair so she falls over. Ouch!

Dame Devin warns Delancy to keep an eye on Blair as the future queen cannot be outshone by a Lady Royal.

At a joint dance class with the Prince Charming Academy, Blair is paired with the coolest, funniest and super-hot prince-to-be, Nicholas. The couple dance flawlessly around the room and can't take their eyes from each other. Nicholas tells Blair she dances beautifully and that he's really looking forward to seeing her again. He kisses her hand goodbye, leaving Blair beaming with delight.

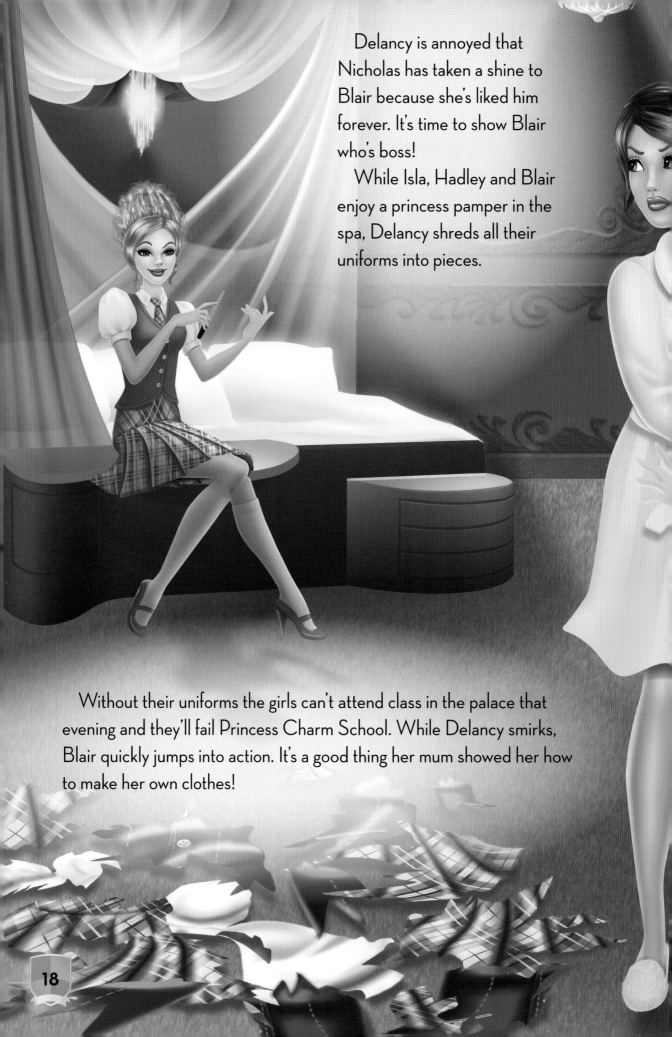

Delancy is annoyed that Nicholas has taken a shine to Blair because she's liked him forever. It's time to show Blair who's boss!

While Isla, Hadley and Blair enjoy a princess pamper in the spa, Delancy shreds all their uniforms into pieces.

Without their uniforms the girls can't attend class in the palace that evening and they'll fail Princess Charm School. While Delancy smirks, Blair quickly jumps into action. It's a good thing her mum showed her how to make her own clothes!

With help from Piper and the other sprites, Blair makes fabulous different uniforms for each of them. Isla and Hadley love how the styles suit their personalities! Blair looks fantastic too – and full of confidence in her new personalized look. The customized outfits look awesome compared to their old uniforms and the girls' princess potential shines through their new clothes. Blair insists that being a princess is not about crowns, it's about character.

Blair, Isla and Hadley get to the palace just in time! Delancy demands that they should still fail the class for wearing the wrong uniform. Blair explains what happened and Headmistress Privet agrees that there is nothing in the school rules against the new clothes, impressed that the girls have unlocked their princess potential. Blair lights up with happiness as her classmates admire her trendy sewing skills.

Before dinner, the students are given a special treat – the chance to explore the palace. Blair, Isla and Hadley set off along a glamorous hall filled with paintings. Nobody sees Delancy sneak along too. Royal secrets, here we come!

Suddenly, Isla spots a beautiful portrait hanging on the wall. The nameplate says 'Queen Isabella, age 18'. The girl in the picture looks just like Blair, but with a sparkly tiara and gorgeous princess gown! How is it possible?

The next painting is of the royal family. Can that be Prince the dog? That must be why he loves Blair more than any other student. Isla and Hadley gasp as Blair reveals she was adopted on the same day as the royal family's accident! Could it be that Blair is actually Queen Isabella's daughter, Princess Anabella? Blair thinks her friends are getting a bit carried away...

As the girls gather for their next class, Dame Devin
announces that when Delancy is queen, she will replace
the poorer areas of Gardania with parkland so the kingdom
is beautiful everywhere. Blair is horrified to see that her
neighbourhood is part of the plan. Even Delancy is too shocked
by her mother's speech and what she found out in the hall of
portraits to say anything.

Dame Devin creates a plan to make sure Blair is expelled from Princess Charm School. She makes Delancy keep watch while she hides some of her jewellery in Blair's room. As the students return, Dame Devin shouts that Blair is a thief and that Delancy saw her steal. A search of the room reveals the hidden jewels and the three friends are told they will be locked up until after the coronation. None of them will wear their crowns! Too afraid of her mother, Delancy keeps silent.

Delancy catches up with the princess prisoners and tells the escorts she wants the pleasure of locking them up herself. The girls are really surprised when Delancy sets them free! Delancy believes Blair is the missing Princess Anabella and wants to help her take her rightful place as queen at the coronation tomorrow. She gives Blair a map of the palace cellar and explains that Gardania's magical crown is in the vault. There's no time to lose!

Blair, Isla and Hadley hurry to the crown jewels and discover the magical crown. Just as Blair is about to open the case, Dame Devin appears with guards and tells her she will never be a princess. Grabbing the crown, Dame Devin leaves them locked in the cellar!

All seems lost, but then Blair realizes Isla keeps humming the same tune. It's the noise the keypad made when Dame Devin locked them in the cellar! Blair quickly links her phone to the door's keypad and asks Isla to sing the tune again. Isla tries several times, but her voice cracks under the pressure. Blair reminds her she's a princess and she can do it. Isla tries once more and the door unlocks with a flourish! Cheering, the girls rush to the coronation. Will they make it in time?

Delancy has been stalling to give Blair more time. Just as she is about to be crowned, she notices Blair run onto the stage. Delancy announces that before she is made ruler for life, it is proper princess protocol that anyone with a claim to the throne must try on the crown. Blair stops to catch her breath and proclaims clearly that she is Princess Anabella, daughter of Queen Isabella, and she claims the throne of Gardania.

Dame Devin is furious, but before she can put the magical crown on Delancy's head, Piper and the sprites whizz through the air and take the crown in a sparkly flash. Delancy gently holds her mother back as the beautiful pink crown is carefully carried closer to Blair's head.

As soon as the magical crown touches Blair, it glows inside out and her outfit blossoms into a wonderful coronation gown. The crowd gasps in awe of Blair's beautiful transformation into Anabella, who radiates princess perfection through the streams of sprite sparkles. She truly is a princess!

Blair steps forward to address her subjects. She proclaims that every girl can find their princess potential, just like her. After crowning Hadley and Isla as princesses, she asks Delancy to be her Lady Royal. Everyone cheers as the girls curtsey to their new Royal Highness.

It's time to party! The room is filled with streamers, disco lights and cool music. All the students of Princess Charm School dance gleefully in their beautiful gowns. The charming Prince Nicholas appears and asks Blair to dance, who happily accepts. There is only one more thing that could make her coronation day perfect...

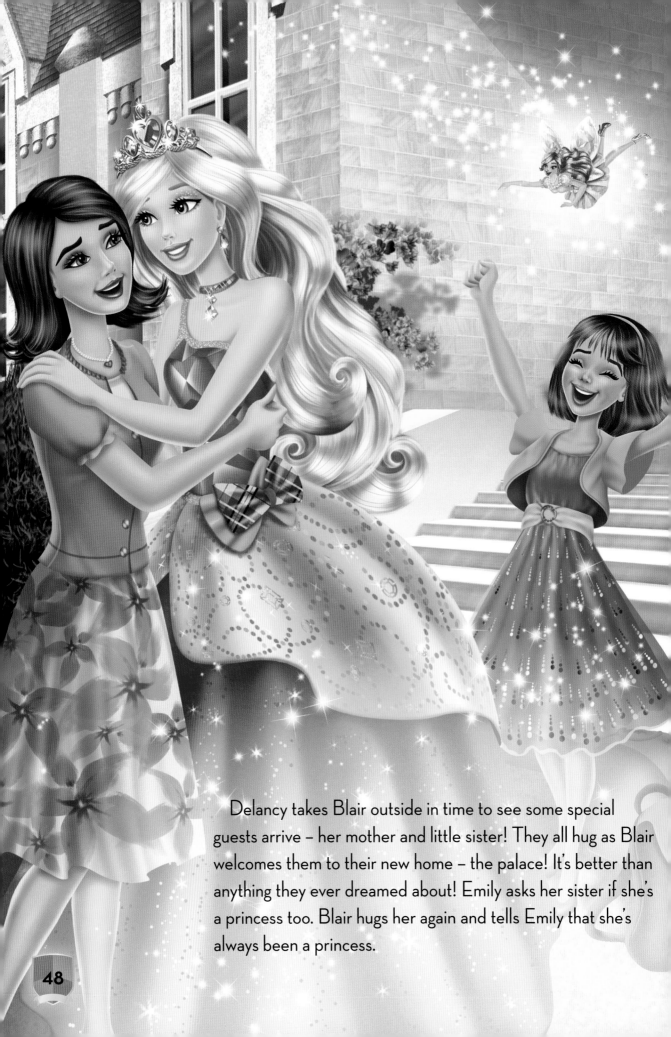

Delancy takes Blair outside in time to see some special guests arrive – her mother and little sister! They all hug as Blair welcomes them to their new home – the palace! It's better than anything they ever dreamed about! Emily asks her sister if she's a princess too. Blair hugs her again and tells Emily that she's always been a princess.